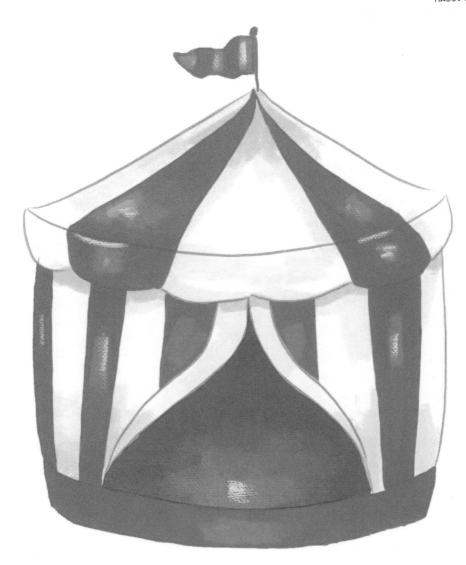

Giggly Bear's
Fun Trip
in the Yellow Bus

Written by Kelly Santana-Banks
Illustrated by Shiela Marie Alejandro

RBTB Publishing

To the safety and well-being of children all over the world.
-K.S. Banks

Published in Coconut Creek, Florida, by RBTB Publishing, an imprint of Reviews by The Banks.

ISBN 978-0-9977530-3-5 (paperback)
ISBN 978-0-9977530-4-2 (hardcover)

Printed in the United Stated of America

Giggly Bear's
Fun Trip
in the Yellow Bus

This book belongs to:

_____

Giggly Bear was excited to go to the funfair

At the school, he was antsy to board the yellow bus.
He almost fell down the stairs.

I am riding in the yellow bus.
I'm having fun with my friend bears.

But safety will always come first.
I'll buckle up to get to the funfair.

The happy bear sat by the window.

His close friend, Tiggy, took the aisle.
The other classmates sat in the back.

The bus driver greeted all with a smile.

I am riding in the yellow bus.
I'm having fun with my friend bears.

But safety will always come first.
I'll buckle up to get to the funfair.

Before leaving the school,
the teacher buckled up the bear students

And made sure they were safely fastened in their seats.

She kindly reminded the bears to stay seated
Or they could get hurt in a heartbeat.

I am riding in the yellow bus.
I'm having fun with my friend bears.

But safety will always come first.
I'll buckle up to get to the funfair.

The group was happy to be on the yellow bus,
So happy that they forgot some rules.

"Look, Tiggy, all the bees!"
Giggly Bear pointed to the hive by the pool.

Tiggy was quick to stand up, but he forgot he was buckled up.

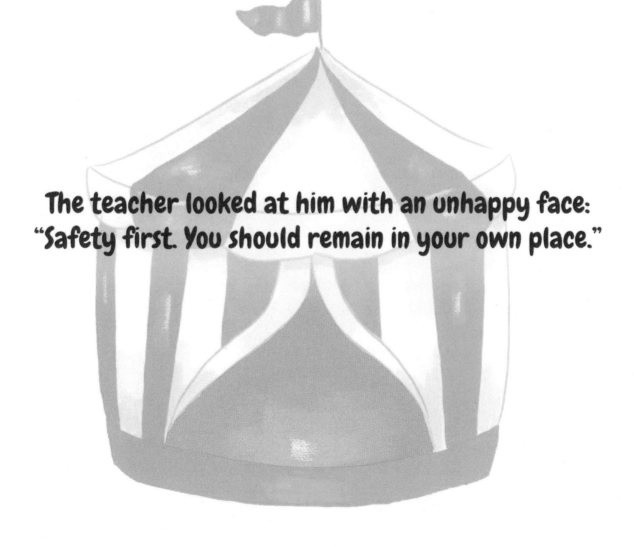

The teacher looked at him with an unhappy face:
"Safety first. You should remain in your own place."

I am riding in the yellow bus.
I'm having fun with my friend bears.

But safety will always come first.
I'll buckle up to get to the funfair

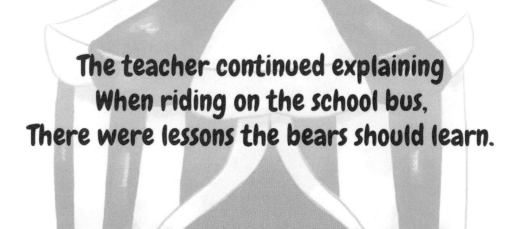

The teacher continued explaining
When riding on the school bus,
There were lessons the bears should learn.

They could get hurt if the bus driver found a pothole . . .
Stopped by surprise . . .
Or even made a sharp turn.

Giggly Bear and Tiggy looked at each other,
making a funny face.
Some of the bears were serious,

I am riding in the yellow bus.
I'm having fun with my friend bears.

But safety will always come first.
I'll buckle up to get to the funfair.

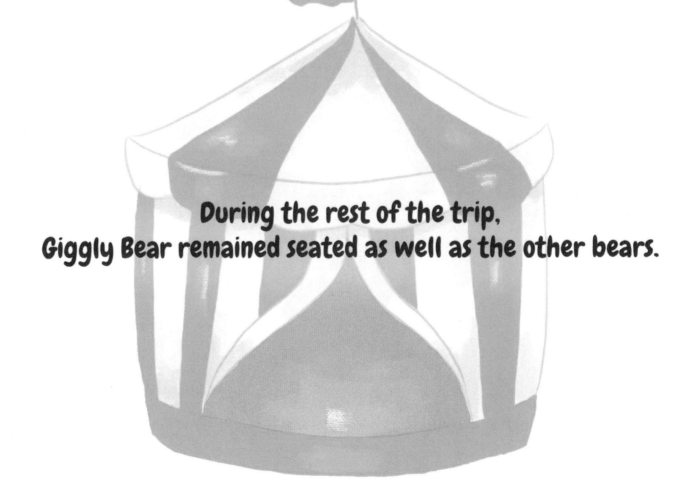

During the rest of the trip,
Giggly Bear remained seated as well as the other bears.

The teacher served yummy snacks

They could not wait to get safely to the funfair.

Do you know?

✔ Around 23.5 million children ride the school bus every year.

✔ Children are seven times safer riding in the school bus than their parent's car.

✔ Approximately 42,000 passengers die every year from crashes on the roads compared to six fatalities a year related to school-aged children riding the school bus.

Safety Tips for Children Riding the Yellow Bus:

✔ While waiting for the school bus, children should stay 6 feet away from the curb.

✔ Children must wait for the bus to come to a full stop and for the driver to signal that it is safe for them to get on the bus.

✔ Children should use a lap or shoulder belt to buckle up (when available).

✔ It is recommended that children use handrails to get on and off the bus.

✔ Children must not walk, cross, or play behind the bus.

✔ When crossing is necessary, children should walk 10 feet away in front of the school bus. It is important that the bus driver sees them and signals that it's safe to cross.

*Resource: National Highway Traffic Safety Administration (NHTSA) / National Safety Council (NSC)

ABOUT THE AUTHOR

Kelly Santana-Banks is a writer of nonfiction and children's books, and a former early childhood teacher and caregiver.

With more than ten years of experience working with children and a strong background in child development, she is an advocate for education, especially in early childhood.

She writes fun stories to entertain and teach children as well as help parents find simple solutions for their little ones' lives.

Giggly Bear's Fun Trip in the Yellow Bus is the third book in the series Let's Learn while Playing. You can find more about her previous titles —The Adventures of Froblicious the Frog and Dinosaur Adventure: A Field Trip to Remember— on her site Reviews by The Banks
(www.reviewsbythebanks.com/books).

You can also connect with her on Twitter @ksantanabanks, Instagram @reviewsbythebanks, or visiting her Facebook page
http://www.facebook.com/ReviewsbytheBanks.

This book was illustrated by Shiela Marie Alejandro from Buckets of Whimsies.

Made in the USA
Middletown, DE
09 August 2019